My Cat Mac

Margaret Forrester and Sandra Klaassen

Picture Kelpies

For Ruth – M.F.

and for Senna and Caj – S.K.

Picture Kelpies is an imprint of Floris Books. First published in 2010 by Floris Books. Second printing 2012. Text © 2010 Margaret Forrester.
Illustrations © 2010 Sandra Klaassen. Margaret Forrester and Sandra Klaassen assert their right under the Copyright,
Designs and Patents Act 1988 to be recognised as the Author and Illustrator of this Work. All rights reserved.
No part of this book may be reproduced without prior permission of
Floris Books, 15 Harrison Gardens, Edinburgh, EH11 1SH www.florisbooks.co.uk
The publisher acknowledges subsidy from Creative Scotland towards the publication of this volume.
British Library CIP Data available. ISBN 978-086315-747-9. Printed in China.

Mac lives in a tall, thin house in Edinburgh. It is his house.
He has lived in it for a long time.

When a new family bought his
house, Mac liked them. He let
them stay.
  There were four
people in the family:
  a mum,
  a dad,
  a friendly boy called Donald
  and a shy, wee girl called Catriona.

"Good," thought Mac. "Maybe Catriona will be my friend.
I have always wanted a special friend."

Catriona thought Mac was wonderful. She picked him up and hugged him so tightly Mac could hardly breathe.

"Put him down, darling," said Mum. "He's real, not a toy."

"I know," said Catriona, and she carried Mac to her bedroom.

Mac sat on Catriona's bed and she showed him all her toys.

"This is my favourite doll, Big Baby. I have a bear, a crocodile and ten koalas too. But none of them is as good as you. You're *real*."

Mac looked interested.

"And this is a pram for Big Baby. You can use it if you like."

Mac did *not* like, but Catriona didn't understand the flick of his tail.

"I've got an idea," she went on. "I'll dress you up and put you in the pram, and we'll go for a walk."

Mac began to growl softly. "I don't like this game," he was saying in cat language. "Please let me go!"

Catriona carried the pram downstairs.
When they reached the kitchen, Mac
leaped out and hid under the table.
  "Whatever are you doing?" cried Mum.
"Take those clothes off him straight away.
He is a *cat*. He is *real*, not a toy."

"He's *my* cat," Catriona muttered, as she ran back up to her room.
Mac took the opportunity to escape through the cat flap.
He wouldn't put up with this!

Mac climbed his favourite lilac tree, lay on his favourite branch and thought to himself:

"I like Catriona better than anyone else. I want her to be my special friend. I have my own fur. I don't need clothes. She must not treat me like that."

So he hatched a plan. He would stay away all night.
Catriona would be worried and would miss him a lot.
But he wouldn't miss her!

Mac went to explore the Water of Leith. He spent all day there.
The river was different from his garden and so were the animals.
"Good evening," Mac said politely as an owl swooped by overhead.
"To you too! To you, to you too!" replied the owl.
Mac hid in the shadows as a hungry fox prowled by.

Soon Mac found that he was getting hungry.

"I wonder what Catriona is doing? Is it time for tea?" he thought.

Mac found that he did miss Catriona after all. "Perhaps I should go back home to make sure she's all right."

While Mac was at the river, Catriona and her family had tea.
 "Mum, can I save my fish for Mac?" asked Catriona.
 Mum smiled. "I think we can spare some for Mac."

Then it was time for bath and bed.

"Mum, can I look for Mac?" asked Catriona.

"He'll be home by morning," Mum said. "Give him time."

She read a bedtime story, kissed Catriona and closed the door.

But Catriona could not sleep. She tossed and turned. Finally she decided she *had* to get up and look for Mac. She put on her slippers and her dressing gown, and tiptoed downstairs.

 She could hear Mum and Dad talking in the sitting room. She tiptoed past the door and slipped out into the garden.

Catriona sat underneath
the old lilac tree and said to
herself, "I'll wait here until
Mac comes, because this is his
favourite place."
 But soon her eyes grew heavy
and she fell asleep.

When Catriona woke up it was dark
and cold and she was shivering.
 "I should get back to bed," she
thought, and hurried to the back door.
But the door would not open.

"Oh no!" Catriona cried. "Mum and Dad have gone to bed and locked the door. I'm shut out." Poor Catriona began to feel lonely and frightened. What was she going to do?

Catriona was so upset, she didn't hear the soft thud as Mac jumped over the garden wall. He tiptoed up to Catriona and licked her face with his rough little tongue, and purred softly in her ear.

"Mac! Oh Mac! You're back. I love you and I'm sorry I dressed you up. But we're locked out."

"Mmmm," thought Mac. "You may be locked out, but I'm not." He bounded towards the back door, jumped through the cat flap, and landed with a gentle plop in the warm dry kitchen.

"Oh," cried Catriona, "I can't squeeze through there!" And she hammered on the back door.

Mac ran through the hall and upstairs until he came to the big bedroom.
Then he let out the biggest, loudest, longest miaow in the whole wide
world. He howled and he yowled. He screamed and he screeched. He
stretched himself up tall and flung himself at the door to push it open.

Dad switched on the bedside light.

"Mac! Stop that noise. You'll wake the neighbours!"

Mac started to yelp again, until both Mum and Dad followed him downstairs. By now Donald had woken up and come down too.

Within seconds, the door was open and Catriona was in Mum's arms.

Soon after that, Catriona was in
dry pyjamas, wrapped in a blanket,
with a mug of hot chocolate. Mac
was enjoying his supper.

"Mac saved me, didn't he, Dad?"

"He certainly did," said Dad.
"But you must never, ever,
go out at night again."

"Mum, can Mac sleep on
my bed tonight?"

"Well," said Mum,
"I don't think we can
make Mac do anything."

"I know, I know. He isn't a doll, he's a *real* cat with *real* feelings. I know that now. Please, Mum? Pleeeease?"

"I'll tell you what ... we'll leave the doors open and see what happens. We'll let Mac decide."

So that is what they did.

Mac finished his supper, thought about everything that had happened, and then made up his mind.

He padded upstairs on velvet paws and curled up on Catriona's bed. And they both slept soundly until morning.